Rumpelstiltskin RETURNS

By Maggie Pearson

Illustrated by Steve Stone

W
FRANKLIN WATTS
LONDON•SYDNEY

Chapter One

As I was walking home from school one day, I heard a voice calling, "Help me!"

I looked around.

There was no one there.

"Help me!" the voice cried.

"Help! This big stone is on top of me!"

I looked down and saw the big stone.
Then I saw a little brown foot
sticking out from under it.

So I rolled that big stone out of the way.
Out popped a funny little man. He looked
like his arms and legs had been made out
of sticks and his hair was like yellow
candy floss.

"You've helped old Rumpelstiltskin,"
the little man said. "Now it's
my turn to help you."
"Help me?" I said. "How?"

"Any way you want! I'm your servant now.
When you've got work to do, I'll do it for
you. From now on you can just have fun."

"What about my mum?" I said. I really wasn't sure what she'd have to say about Rumpelstiltskin moving in with us.

"She won't see me," he said.

"Nobody will. It will be our secret."

"All right," I said. "It's a deal!"

"Just don't ever thank me. I hate it if people say thank you!" Rumpelstiltskin said.

Then, in a flash of light, he was gone.

Chapter Two

"Tidy your room!" Mum called out as I went up the stairs.

I smiled to myself. Time to call on Rumpelstiltskin.

But Rumpelstiltskin had got there ahead
of me. Everything was so neat and tidy,
it didn't look like my room at all.

I got out my homework. Today it
was maths. I'm rubbish at maths.
Rumpelstiltskin had done it for me!

Next day at school, I got ten out of ten for my homework. But the teacher didn't think I'd done it all by myself. I had to stay in at playtime and do it all over again, so she could watch me do it. I still got the answers right, luckily!

After school we played football. I'm usually rubbish at football. That day I scored goal after goal.

No one could get the ball off me. Whenever I aimed for the goal, the ball went in.

GOAL!

GOAL!

I knew it was Rumpelstiltskin doing it. But nobody else could see him.

In the end everyone got fed up and went home. I was angry so I shouted out, "Rumpelstiltskin! I want a word with you! When I want your help, I'll ask for it."

"No need to ask," he said.
"I do all the work.
You have all the fun.
That was our deal."

"Football is fun!" I said.

"It looked more like hard work to me," he replied.

Chapter Three

Every day Rumpelstiltskin made my bed and cleaned my shoes.

He tidied my room and he did my homework.

16

He weeded the garden and mowed the lawn.

He washed up for Dad.

He cleaned the car for Mum.

My parents thought I was doing it all. They told all their friends about me. And I was top of the class.

But nobody likes a goody-goody. Nobody likes a teacher's pet. I was losing all my friends.

"Rumpelstiltskin!" I yelled. "I don't want you to be my servant any more."

"You said I could be your servant if I wanted," he said. "And I do. I want to be your servant forever!"

I didn't want Rumpelstiltskin to be my servant for ever and ever. What could I do?

Chapter Four

There had to be something I could do on my own, where Rumpelstiltskin couldn't help me. Perhaps then he'd leave me alone.

I thought about it.

I thought and thought.

One day, I had an idea! I entered for a
summer fun run. I'm rubbish at running.
I knew I couldn't win. And Rumpelstiltskin
couldn't make me.

He'd have to pick me up and carry me if he wanted me to win. Then people would see him. I didn't think he wanted that.

Chapter Five

The day of the race came.

The starter raised his pistol.

Ready,

steady,

– GO!

Two of the runners fell over their own feet.

Someone had tied their laces together –

guess who!

Then two runners started fighting.

Each of them said the other had punched

him in the ribs. I knew who it really was.

Another was stung by
a wasp and had to go
to the first aid tent.
This didn't look good.

I set off with the rest of the runners, following the signs, down the path and into the woods.

I passed runners who'd lost a shoe in the mud and others who'd sprained their ankles or tripped over and grazed their knees.

I saw signs swing round, then back again after the runners ahead of me had turned the wrong way.

In the end I stopped and sat down.

"Rumpelstiltskin!" I yelled.

"I'm not moving till you promise
to let me finish this race by myself.
No more tricks! I can do this on my own,
thanks very much. I don't need any help
from you."

"What did you say?" asked Rumpelstiltskin.
"You said 'Thanks very much'. Didn't I
tell you not to thank me?" he yelled.
"If there's one thing I can't stand it's
people thanking me!"

He stamped his foot.
"I won't be thanked!
I won't! I won't!
You'll get no more help
from Rumpelstiltskin!"

29

He started spinning round and round.

"You can tidy your own room and do

your own homework!" he yelled.

He was spinning so fast now,

he was just a blur.

Then, in a flash, he was gone.

I could still hear him shouting,

"You'll never see Rumpelstiltskin again!"

"Thanks very much!" I yelled back,

just to make sure that I never did.

First published in 2012 by
Franklin Watts
338 Euston Road
London
NW1 3BH

Franklin Watts Australia
Level 17/207 Kent Street
Sydney
NSW 2000

Text © Maggie Pearson 2012
Illustration © Steve Stone 2012

The rights of Maggie Pearson to be
identified as the author and Steve Stone as
the illustrator of this Work have been
asserted in accordance with the Copyright,
Designs and Patents Act, 1988.

Series Editor: Melanie Palmer
Series Advisor: Catherine Glavina
Series Designer: Peter Scoulding

A CIP catalogue record for this book is
available from the British Library.

ISBN 978 1 4451 0776 9 (hbk)
ISBN 978 1 4451 0782 0 (pbk)

Printed in China

Franklin Watts is a division of Hachette
Children's Books, an Hachette UK company.
www.hachette.co.uk